WILD ACTION NEWS
REPORTER TO THE RESCUE

by J.L. Anderson
illustrated by Amanda Erb

Rourke
Educational Media
rourkeeducationalmedia.com

A Division of
Carson
Dellosa
Education

Dear Guardian/Educator,

Introduce your child to the wonderful world of reading with our leveled readers. Your growing reader will be continuously engaged as he or she is guided from one level to the next. Each level is carefully built to provide your child with the reading skills and knowledge to be a confident reader! Ultimately, we want your child to develop a love of reading.

Level 1 *Learning to Read*
High frequency words, basic sentences, large type, labels, full color illustrations to help young readers better comprehend the text

Level 2 *Beginning to Read Alone*
Short sentences, familiar words, simple plot, easy-to-read fonts

Level 3 *Reading on Your Own*
Short paragraphs, easy-to-follow plots, vocabulary is increasingly challenging, exciting stories

Level 4 *Proficient Reader*
Chapters, engaging stories, challenging vocabulary, multiple text features

Reading should be a pleasurable experience. A child who enjoys reading reads more, and a child who reads more becomes a better reader. Your child will grow with exposure to broad vocabulary and literary techniques, and will develop deeper critical thinking and comprehension skills. We are excited to be a part of your child's reading journey.

Happy reading,
Rourke Educational Media

Library of Congress PCN Data

Reporter to the Rescue / J.L. Anderson
(WILD Action News)
ISBN 978-1-73161-497-1 (hard cover)(alk. paper)
ISBN 978-1-73161-304-2 (soft cover)
ISBN 978-1-73161-602-9 (e-Book)
ISBN 978-1-73161-707-1 (ePub)
Library of Congress Control Number: 2019932405

Edited by: Kim Thompson
Cover and interior layout by: Rhea Magaro-Wallace
Cover and interior illustrations by: Amanda Erb

Table of Contents

Chapter One
Swoop for the Scoop

I hear a rumble. Was that a growl? There could be trouble. I need the **scoop**!

Table of Contents

Chapter One
Swoop for the Scoop

I hear a rumble. Was that a growl? There could be trouble. I need the **scoop**!

I'm Bald Eagle. I'm part of

the WILD Action News team.

I fly out of my nest to **investigate**.

My eyes are sharp. I see everything in color.

When I'm not hunting for food, my eyes help me find news stories.

That's what reporters do! We hunt down the news.

The forest is green.

The lake is bright blue.

It's full of fish. I love fish!

But there is no time to eat.
I need to find a **source** for
my story. Hmm...what is that
brown thing down there?

Chapter Two
What's the Story?

It's Beaver! "Hello, Beaver,"
I call as I swoop down. I don't
want to scare her. "Did you
hear that roar?"

Beaver doesn't say anything.

But there is no time to eat.
I need to find a **source** for
my story. Hmm...what is that
brown thing down there?

What's the Story?

It's Beaver! "Hello, Beaver,"
I call as I swoop down. I don't
want to scare her. "Did you
hear that roar?"

Beaver doesn't say anything.

"Please trust me. I'm not going to eat you," I say.

Beaver moves forward. She looks right, then left. "Okay. I did hear a roar," she whispers.

"What did it sound like?

Where did it come from?"

I ask.

Every reporter needs to

ask questions: *What? Where?*

When? Who? Why? How?

Reporters ask questions to
gather facts. They share the
facts with others. Reporters
keep everyone informed!

"It sounded like a bear.

Or maybe a mountain lion,"

Beaver says.

"Are you sure?" I ask.

Beaver tries to make a roaring sound. She sounds like a baby crying.

I try not to laugh. News is serious business.

"My eyes may not see as well as yours, but my ears are fine," Beaver says.

She points to a mountain. "The roar came from over there," she says.

Beaver tries to make a roaring sound. She sounds like a baby crying.

I try not to laugh. News is serious business.

"My eyes may not see as well as yours, but my ears are fine," Beaver says.

She points to a mountain. "The roar came from over there," she says.

"Thanks!" I say. I fly away.

ROAR!

I hear it louder now. I'm

getting close!

Chapter Three
A Scoop with a Twist

I spy a brown animal MUCH

larger than Beaver. She's

strong with big shoulders.

It's Grizzly Bear. Her claws
are twice the size of my talons.
She growls again.

I have questions. I need answers! "Why are you growling? Who else is here?"

Grizzly Bear charges a human's cabin. I see a baby bear by her side.

I've done some **research**

on grizzly bears. They usually

have two or three cubs.

Did something happen to
one of her babies? I swoop
lower to get a better look.

A cub is on the cabin's porch. It has a trash can stuck on its head. Bears look for food everywhere.

Even humans' trash cans!

This is bad. The cub could get hurt by a human. Or Grizzly Bear could hurt a human to protect her cubs. They need to get out of here fast!

A reporter's job is to report the story, not be part of the story. But in this case, these bears need help!

I swoop in. I use my beak and talons to save the cub.

"Thank you!" Grizzly Bear
calls as she runs away with
her cubs.

This is the first time I've
been the hero of my own
news report.

And I have the perfect

headline!

Bonus Stuff!

Glossary

headline (HED-line): The title of a newspaper or news website article.

investigate (in-VES-ti-gate): To gather information.

research (REE-surch): To collect information about a topic through reading, investigating, or experimenting.

scoop (skoop): A story reported by a news organization before other news organizations have reported it.

source (sors): A person who gives information.

Discussion Questions

1. What are some things that Bald Eagle does to get the scoop on the mysterious growl?
2. Is Bald Eagle a good reporter? Why or why not?
3. How and why did Bald Eagle become part of the story he was reporting?

Activity:
Comic Book Artist

A comic book tells a story in a series of panels. Each panel is a box that contains pictures of the characters and the words they say.

Make a comic book about Grizzly Bear. First, use a pencil and a ruler to draw a series of boxes on sheets of paper. Use a pencil to fill the panels with drawings, speech bubbles, and words. Create the comic from Grizzly Bear's point of view. Tell her side of the story. Include Beaver, Bald Eagle, the cubs, humans, or other characters you might meet in the forest.

Use colored pencils or markers to color your panels. Share your comic book with family and friends.

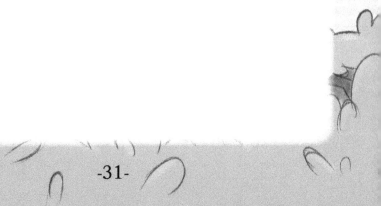

Writing Prompt

Write Bald Eagle's news story. Be sure to answer who, what, when, where, why, and how. What photographs might be included with the story? Draw them.

About the Author

J.L. Anderson is always curious to get the scoop! She loves writing for kids of all ages, and she's passionate about animals and nature. You can learn more about her by visiting www.jessicaleeanderson.com.

About the Illustrator

Amanda is always on the lookout for new stories to illustrate! Some of her favorite stories to illustrate involve expressive animal and human characters. You can find more of her work at www.amandaerb.com.

CPSIA information can be obtained
at www.ICGtesting.com
Printed in the USA
JSHW050809080522
25660JS00001B/1